Vikram and Betaal

Four Suitors

& Other Stories

MAPLE PRESS

FOUR SUITORS & OTHER STORIES

Price: ₹ 25/-

Reprinted in 2017 by

MAPLE PRESS PRIVATE LIMITED
sales office A-63, Sector 58, Noida 201301, U.P., India
phone +91 120 455 3581, 455 3583
email : info@maplepress.co.in
website : www.maplepress.co.in
          : www.maplelibrary.com

ISBN: 978-93-50335-22-2

Printed at HT Media Ltd., Noida

King Vikramaditya Meets Betaal

Many years ago a king called Vikramaditya lived in India. He was known for his wisdom and kindness. But people talked about his bravery.

One day, in the court of the king a strange tantric came and presented him with a fruit. The king accepted the fruit. The strange tantric asked the king to keep the fruit in his treasury.

The tantric again came to the king's court the next day and again presented a fruit. This continued for many years until one day the treasurer came to the court told the king about a mysterious happening.

The king left the court immediately and rushed to his treasury. The fruits that the tantric had been presenting to the king over the years had all turned into precious stones. The king and his ministers were overjoyed. They could not believe their eyes.

The next day, when the tantric arrived, the king stood from his throne and bowed to him with respect and said—

"O great saint, it is indeed an honour that my court should be graced with your presence. What can I do in return for your blessings? "

The tantric said, "My blessings shall always be with you wise king. But there is something that I must ask you to do."

The great king had never turned away anyone who came to his court seeking his help. He agreed to fulfill the tantric's wish.

The tantric said "Deep in the forest, where most people fear to go, there is a Peepal tree on which hangs the body of a dead man. You must bring me that dead body. I have to offer that corpse to the Goddess for her blessings. You must go to the forest alone, on the next new moon night."

The king started for the Pandabaranya forest at once. As directed by the tantric, he began looking for the Peepal tree that stood in the centre of the forest. It was dark inside the forest. But Vikramaditya was brave. He moved on.

The night set in and there was no moon in the sky. The king approached the Peepal tree with sword in his hand. Skulls, skeletons and bones were scattered on the ground under the tree. From a distance, the king saw the dead body. It was thin and white as chalk and hung upside down from a branch.

The king climbed the tree. With great effort, he dragged the corpse through the branches and climbed down from

the tree. He then put the corpse around his shoulders and
began walking towards home. Suddenly the dead body
began laughing. It was ghost.

The king was shocked but he was not scared. He calmly

continued his journey.

The ghost asked, "Who are you?" The king replied, "I'm king Vikramaditya." He asked the ghost "Who are you?" The ghost said, "I am Betaal. Where are you taking me?"

The king told Betaal about the tantric and how he had requested the king to bring Betaal to him. Betaal did not seem surprised. He said, "He is a fraud. I was born on the same day and at the same hour as the tantric. If the tantric gets me, he will use me to increase his powers and then he will kill you to increase his powers further."

The king was in distress. "I have already promised the Tantric that I would bring you to him. It would not be fair if I failed. I must carry you to him even if my life is at stake," he said. Betaal was impressed with the king. He decided to help him.

He said, "All right then, I will tell you a story at the end of which I will ask you a question. If your answer is wrong, I will come with you. But if you answer it correctly, I will fly back to the tree. However if you choose to be silent, your head will burst into flames. Do you agree?"

Betaal knew that the wise king will always know the answer and he will never lie. Vikramaditya had no choice but to agree. Betaal began to tell a story.

Four Suitors

Once upon a time a wise king named Udayaditya lived in Mithila. Everyone under his rule respected the king for his sense of justice and equality. They loved him for his kindness.

The king had a daughter. She was known for her beauty and intelligence. Rumours said that princess Rupamanjari was so beautiful that she could make any man fall in love with her.

When she grew up, all the eligible princes in the kingdoms near and far wished to marry her. It was hard for the poor king and his queen to select which of them would be best for their beloved daughter.

Then one day, while the king held the royal court, a very handsome prince approached him and bowed respectfully and said is a deep voice, "I am the prince of Kalinga and I have come to you with a wish in my heart." He said that he desired to marry the princess.

The king said, "I respect your wish young man. Kalinga is our neighbor and ally. I shall be happy to have you as my son-in-law as this shall strengthen the bonds between our kingdoms. But tell me, apart from belonging to a royal family, what do you think makes you special?"

The prince said, "Your majesty, I am a warrior and I have trained with great masters, in various forms of martial arts. I lead the army of my country as their chief and have won many battles." The king was pleased. He invited the young prince to stay with his family in the palace as a royal guest until the princess made a decision about the proposal.

Next day, as the king was holding his court, another young prince approached him and said that he wished to marry the princess. This young prince introduced himself as the prince of Janakpura and said, "Your majesty, I have read all the religious books. I have spent days searching for the truths of life and of the world. My quest for knowledge makes me special." The king was impressed again. He requested the prince to stay as his royal guest until it was decided.

On the third day, another handsome prince approached the king and said he was from Vaishali. He too said that he wished to marry princess Rupamanjari. He said, "Your majesty, I am gifted by mother nature. I can understand the language of birds and beasts. I understand their joys and their sorrows." The king admired his talent. Like before, he asked this prince too to remain as his guest while the princess made a decision about the proposal.

And there on the fourth day came to the king a prince from Malabya. Like all the three princes who came before him, he too expressed his desire to marry the princess. He claimed, "Your majesty, I come from a rich kingdom where we believe that progress lies in making money. I am a skilled trader. I can make good use of wealth to generate more wealth."

The king and his queen were confused as to which prince amongst the four would make a perfect groom for their daughter. After much thought, they left it to their daughter to decide.

And here, Betaal stopped. He asked, "Great king, now tell me, who do you think should the princess choose? Who should make the right match for her beauty and intelligence?"

Vikramaditya was quick to answer, "If the princess is as intelligent as you tell me, she would select the prince of Kalinga. The prince of Janakpura is a scholar. He cannot be a good king." Betaal nodded. The king continued, "The prince from Vaishali is exceptionally gifted as he can understand the language of the birds and the beasts. But what good is that when his kingdom is at war? And as for the prince of Malabya, he by virtue is a businessman and no king. If the princess is wise and cares for her people, she would marry the prince of Kalinga as he is a true warrior and during times of war, he will lead his people to peace."

Betaal was laughing again. "You are right, great king. And here I go." With a swift tug, Betaal freed himself from Vikramaditya and flew back to the tree.

The Two Gifted Brothers

Betaal was gleefully swinging from his bough when Vikramaditya reached him and dragged him down from the tree. Putting Betaal around his shoulders he continued his journey.

The thin clouds silently parted in the sky and the stars twinkled from between them. Betaal sighed. He asked, "You don't give up easily. Do you?" The king smiled. Betaal began to tell another story.

Once upon a time a scholarly Brahmin lived in the city of Pataliputra. He was a gentle and a very pious man. God had blessed him with two sons. Both of them were as gentle and kind as their father. These two sons were extraordinarily talented.

The elder son was gifted with the ability to judge people's character and by so doing could warn the others of their intensions. The younger brother had the ability judge the nature of things by smelling them.

The talents of the two brothers began to be much talked about in the kingdom. The king heard of this and one day they were called to the court.

The king wished to employ them as his special advisors. The brothers agreed.

They began to assist the king in all his decisions. They would often travel with the king on his diplomatic visits to other kingdoms.

One day, while on one such visit, the king and his party were given a warm welcome by the kingdom. A festival and several programmes were organized in their honour.

The king and his men feasted on the food and wine all night and after that the king wished to take rest. The large royal guest room was richly furnished for him. The king after having a heavy meal wanted nothing but to lay his head on the pillow and close his eyes for a bit.

He entered the room with the brothers behind him. The elder brother said, "Your majesty, I do not trust the king of this kingdom. He is jealous of you and plots to kill you."

The king said, "Nonsense! He has arranged so much to make us comfortable. I don't see how he may be plotting to harm me. I think too much food is making you mad." Then he sat on his bed and leaned to grab the pillow when the elder brother caught his wrist.

"Pardon me your majesty, but I think something is wrong. We must have that pillow checked before you lay your head on it."

The king was confused and irritated. But he could not ignore the elder brother's warning. He asked the younger

brother to inspect the pillow. The younger brother who
was standing at the door came closer and sniffed the
pillow.

The younger brother said, "The pillow is laced with
animal hair your highness. Some of those are pretty sharp

and shall cut through your skin if you lie on it. The tips are laced with poison that can kill you."

The king did not touch the pillow. He decided to spend the rest of the night without a pillow and next morning he secretly carried the pillow with him and returned to his own kingdom. When he had it checked by experts, they told him that the brothers had been correct. He rewarded the brothers handsomely for their service.

Betaal continued, "Tell me great king, which of the two brothers was wiser and had the greater talent?"

The king smiled. He knew the answer this time too. He said, "The elder one. He was the one who sensed the wrong intentions of their host. He was the one who suspected the pillow first. The younger brother only used his talents to confirm his brother's suspicion."

Betaal was shaking with laughter. He had begun to enjoy the game. He said, "Your judgment is flawless," And he rose and flew back to his tree. An owl hooted and it echoed through the forest.

Ranjabati's Dilemma

Once again, king Vikramaditya climbed the tree and brought Betaal down. Crickets screeched from the bushes and the cool night breeze brushed past them. Lifelessly swinging on the king's shoulder, Betaal began to tell another story.

A rich merchant lived in the capital city of Magadha. He was called Bidhushekhar. Bidhushekhar was known within his community for his wealth and honourable living. He had a son named Rajshekhar.

Rajshekhar had grown up with another young boy called Aviroop. They had always been best friends. People who did not know about them often thought that they were brothers.

As they grew up to be young men, they began to enjoy themselves by travelling in and around the city. One day as they were relaxing on the banks of the river which ran by a temple of Goddess Durga, Rajshekhar spotted a very beautiful girl. He fell in love with her at once.

Aviroop knew who the girl was. He himself had been in love with her for a very long time now. He told his friend that her name was Ranjabati and she belonged to the washerman community.

They began to visit that place every day. Rajshekhar's heart pined for Ranjabati. Aviroop suggested, "Why don't you tell your parents about her?"

Rajshekhar sadly lowered his eyes and said "They will never understand. They will never agree that I marry a girl from a caste lower to my own. I fear that it will only make them angry." Aviroop felt very sorry for his friend.

Day by day Rajshekhar's love for Ranjabati grew. When he could not take it anymore, he went to the temple and fell at Goddess Durga's feet. "Mother, my love for Ranjabati is killing me. Bless me mother, that I marry Ranjabati. I promise I shall offer you my head on a full moon night."

He began to waste away in love. He stopped eating and his bones began to show. His sickness worried his parents. They wondered what had happened to their son. Aviroop told them that Rajshekhar had fallen in love with Ranjabati and was wasting away because he couldn't marry her without their consent.

Afraid that they might lose their only son Bidhushekhar and his wife agreed to marry Rajshekhar to Ranjabati. The wedding was arranged and the feast continued for the next few days. Rajshekhar recovered from his illness

and they lived happily together.

One day when Rajshekhar, Ranjabati and Aviroop were visiting the river where they had first seen Ranjabati, Rajshekhar remembered his promised to Goddess Durga.

He decided to wait for a full moon night.

As the next full moon night arrived, he went to the temple. With folded hands and tears in his eyes he thanked the Goddess for her blessings. Then with his sword, he cut his head off.

When Rajshekhar did not come back, Ranjabati began to worry. She sent Aviroop to look for her husband. When Aviroop found his friend in the temple he grieved. He prayed to the Goddess, "Mother, I do not want people to believe that I have murdered my best friend for his beautiful wife. I must also offer myself to you. Please accept my sacrifice." And with Rajshekhar's sword, he cut his head from his body and lay there at the Goddess's feet.

Ranjabati after waiting for a long time grew impatient. She set out herself to find her husband and his friend. When she reached the temple she almost fainted to see the men lying in a pool of blood.

She prayed, "Mother, since my husband is no more in this world I do not have any purpose left." As she was about to plunge the sword into her chest, there was a mysterious light and the Goddess appeared.

"Dear girl, I am very pleased with the sacrifices of these humble men. Do not kill yourself. I shall return their lives to you. As soon as you place their heads on their bodies, they will come back to life."

Goddess Durga disappeared. Overwhelmed with joy,

Ranjabati placed the heads on the bodies and the men came back to life. But in her excitement, Ranjabati had exchanged the heads, placing Aviroop's head on Rajshekhar's body and Rajshekhar's head on Aviroop's body.

Betaal said, "Great king, who do you think should Ranjabati take for her husband?"

The king was lost in thoughts. "Ranjabati should choose the body with Rajshekhar's head. Head is most important as it holds a man's personality, character and identity."

Betaal knew the king would answer it wisely. "You are right again," he said and he laughed as he flew towards the tree.

The Learned Fools and A Lion

Once upon a time there lived a poor Brahmin in a small village near Benaras. He had four sons. All of them were foolish and lazy. Though everybody in the village respected the Brahmin, they laughed at him behind his back because of his sons were good for nothing.

This made the Brahmin sad. He decided that his sons must be educated and soon he arranged to send them to a very learned teacher. The four lazy brothers lived with their teacher and studied the scriptures, until they became learned men themselves.

When the four Brahmin sons had completed their course of study, they left their home to travel far and wide. They walked till the edge of the village and entered the forest. They decided to cross it. When they reached the middle of the forest, it was mid day and they were tired and hungry.

They sat down under a large tree and opened their luggage for food and water. Then one of them noticed a skull and few bones that were scattered around the tree. They began to wonder.

The eldest brother said, "I will find out what was the animal that died here." And he began to chant mantras. The bones began to move. They joined each other and formed the skeleton of a lion.

"It's a lion!" the second brother exclaimed. "I will put some flesh on it so that we are sure." And he began to chant mantras. Flesh appeared on the skeleton and it was clear that it was a lion.

The third brother, now eager to show them the wonders he could do said, "Let me put skin on the animal so that we are absolutely sure that it is a lion." He sat crossed legged and chanted mantras. Skin magically appeared on the flesh. The brother continued, until golden fur and a thick mane appeared on the animal. Everyone was impressed.

The lion stood with his eyes closed. It was now the youngest brother's turn. He thought of a plan. "Dear brothers, what I can do will truly amaze you," and by saying so he closed his eyes and chanted the mantras he knew.

The lion sprang to life. It roared loudly. The four brothers could do nothing as the hungry lion pounced on them one by one and ate them up.

Betaal asked, "Dear king, who do you believe was the most foolish of the four brothers?"

The king answered, "No doubt all the four brothers were very foolish. But the youngest was the most foolish of them all. When his brothers had made the lion, he should have sensed the danger in bringing the lion back to life. But he was too eager to show his talent. It was his lack of judgment which got all of them killed."

Without a word, Betaal flew back to the tree. The king had been right. Betaal now truly admired the king for his wisdom.

An Example of Generosity

King Vikramaditya was getting tired of Betaal's game but he was determined to take Betaal with him even if he had to spend the night climbing up and down the tree. He put Betaal around his shoulders again and set on his journey.

Betaal was enjoying himself very much. "How long do you wish to keep this up?" he asked. "It depends on you," the king answered. Betaal shook with laughter. "All right, I will begin the story then."

Long ago, there lived a rich merchant named Chandrapati in a city called Mahabalipur. He had a beautiful daughter named Madhumala. One day Madhumala was attending a social event when a handsome young man named Aditya saw her and fell in love with her. Madhumala too was charmed by the young man's sweet nature and wit.

Their love grew with time until one day Aditya decided to marry Madhumala. He went to her father seeking his permission and blessings. But Chandrapati had already promised to wed his daughter to a wealthy young merchant named Sarbajyoti. Aditya was heart-broken.

After days of living with the sorrow, he finally decided to forget Madhumala. However, Madhumala who had loved Aditya could not do so. She silently protested against her father's wishes. But Madhumala had to marry Sabrajyoti for had she not she would have earned her family a bad name.

The day before the marriage took place, she wrote to Aditya promising him that she will come to him after the marriage and shall live with him thereafter. On the night she was alone with her husband for the first time, Madhumala opened her heart to Sarbajyoti and told him everything. Sarbajyoti realised that there was no use trying to persuade her as she already loved someone else. He allowed her to leave.

Madhumala left her home still dressed in her bridal saree and ornaments. On her way a thief crossed her path. "Give me all your jewels or I will hurt you," he threatened. "Please let me go good sir," Madhumala begged. "I am in a hurry to go to my lover. I promise I will give you all my jewels when I have met him." The thief did not believe her but he let her go.

Madhumala reached Aditya's home and knocked on the door. Aditya appeared at the door and was pretty shocked to see Madhumala. He was angry that she had left her husband to come to him. "What were you thinking? You

are a married woman now. I cannot have someone else's
wife to live with me. You must go back to your husband.
There is no place for you here." And he closed the door
on her.

Madhumala begged and cried in vain. At last with a heavy heart she decided to go back. On her way she met the thief again. She began to unhook her jewels to give to him.

The thief had noticed her tears. He asked, "What bothers you lady?" Madhumala told him the whole story. The thief was sorry for her. He did not take her jewels and saw that she safely reached her home.

When Madhumala reached home Sarbajyoti was upset upon seeing her. He said, "I am sorry, I cannot have you back as my wife. You left my home to live to another man. I do not trust you anymore and thus cannot have you back. You must leave."

All hell broke loose for Madhumala. She now had nowhere to go. Fearing the shame that this would bring her she went to the river nearby and ended her life.

Betaal stopped. He asked, "Who do you think made the greatest sacrifice?"

The king replied, "It is only when you give up something willingly and selflessly it is called a sacrifice. Aditya gave up Madhumala's love but he did it for a reason. Madhumala was somebody's wife and he could not have somebody's wife living with him. Sarbajyoti let go of Madhumala but he would not have her back because he did not trust her. Madhumala on the other hand gave up her life but it was because she was afraid of the shame her condition would bring her. We cannot call these as sacrifices. Only the thief made the sacrifice. Robbing people was how he earned his livelihood. But he let go of Madhumala's jewels because he took pity in her. His act of humanity truly sets an example of what sacrifice is."

"I was expecting that you would give me the right answer," Betaal said. Vikramaditya turned around and began walking towards the tree as the ghost flew back to its branches.

King Bhoja Finds Vikramaditya's Throne

After many such attempts, it was Betaal who was forced to give up and go to the tantric with Vikramaditya. The story of king Vikramaditya and Betaal, went down in history as one of the greatest examples of patience, determination and wisdom.

Many years later, a king called Bhoja, who ruled over the great city of Ujjaini was told about this great king. However, it was interesting, how he found out about king Vikramaditya.

Many years after king Vikramaditya's rule, the great king Bhoja, who ruled the city of Ujjaini went hunting in the forests around his city with some of his men. The wild animals from the forests were disturbing the peace of some villages nearby. So the king decided to kill the animals and restore the peace.

They had spent all day in the forest chasing the animals. When it was mid day and the sun began to shine mightily above them, they decided to rest for a while. They began looking for a spot to rest.

After searching for a long time, they came across a large field. The corn that grew in that field looked delicious. The king was impressed. He began to look for the owner.

They spotted him sitting at the center of the field, on a mound of earth. When they approached him, he stood up and bowed. "I am honoured that you have graced my fields with your presence, your majesty. I am Saravana Bhatta and I own these fields. Please feel free to rest and feast on the corn."

The king and his men were delighted. They set up camp in the field and began to feast on the sweet, juicy corn.

When Saravana Bhatta got down from the mound and saw that the king and his men were feasting on his crops he grew furious. He went to the king and said, "Your majesty, I am a poor man. This corn is my livelihood. If you and your men eat my crop how will I feed my family?" The king offered Saravana Bhatta some money in return for his favour. The farmer thanked the king and went back to his mound.

Strangely when the farmer sat on the mound again, he said, "Your majesty, you rule over these lands. These are more your fields than mine and these are your crops. I am disappointed that you should pay me for what belongs to you. I refuse to take this money." And he returned the

money to the king.

The king was now confused. He realised, there was something wrong with the mound. He offered to buy the field from Saravana Bhatta. After having paid a huge price, he ordered the mound to be dug. To everyone's astonishment, the men discovered a large golden throne buried in the mound.

It was a beautiful peacock throne. It was made of solid gold and was studded with precious stones and thirty two strange looking dolls. The king fell in love with the throne at once. He wished it to be carried back to the palace.

But they could not move the throne. The king ordered for more men. But the throne seemed to be magical. It got heavier and heavier making it impossible to be moved. Then one wise advisor suggested, "Your majesty, this throne seemed to have belonged to a great king. We must worship the throne before trying to move it." The king agreed and a team of Brahmins were called who performed a ritual around the throne. It helped and the throne finally moved.

They brought the throne to the palace and on an auspicious day, the king having finished his morning duties decided to sit on the throne. However no sooner had he stepped on the pedestal, one of the dolls started laughing very loudly. "Wait O king, do you think you have got what it takes to sit on this throne?"

The king was taken by surprise. He said, "Pardon me, I do not understand." "This throne had belonged to the great king Vikramaditya. It takes only greatness like his to sit on this throne. Do you think your wisdom and justice matches that of great king Vikramaditya?"

"Tell me. How great was king Vikramaditya? I want to know more about him" Bhoja demanded.

The doll laughed, "I will tell you a story and you shall judge for yourself, how great king Vikramaditya was." And the doll began to tell a story about king Vikramaditya's greatness. King Bhoja sat wide eyed as he heard the story. He realised, his wisdom and justice were no match for Vikramaditya. King Vikramaditya was indeed a great king.